Whooooo, whoooo does this book belong to?

_____

_____

M. D. ANDERSON CANCER CENTER
Children's Art Project™

The Children's Art Project at The University of Texas M. D. Anderson Cancer Center
began in 1973 with a mission of making life better for children with cancer. The volunteer-
driven project blends business and caring to do just that. Through worldwide sales of young
cancer patients' artwork featured on seasonal note cards and gifts, the project has funded
educational programs, college scholarships, summer camps, ski trips, the Child Life program
and other exciting activities that benefit cancer patients and their families.

Our Shadow Garden

by Cherie Foster Colburn

Art by the children of the Children's Cancer Hospital
at M. D. Anderson Cancer Center

Many people have gardens...

Some people grow vegetable gardens with corn and carrots.

Some people grow fruits like peaches and pears.

Some people grow flowers like daisies and dahlias.

But I don't know anyone else who has a shadow garden.

Gardening: the quick cure for what ails you!

• Did you know that doctors found being in a garden or even just seeing one can make your heart beat slower, keep you from getting a cold, and help you feel less afraid?

• People in the hospital get well faster when they see trees out their window than when they just see a brick wall.

• Looking at flowers and smelling them helps your mind stop worrying because you are waking up your senses and distracting your brain.

• If you do not have a place for your own outside garden, an inside plant can make you feel better by cleaning the air as it "breathes" in the stale air in your house and gives you fresh air.

My grandfather Poppa and I built our shadow garden for my grandmother Nana last summer. She got sick, and the doctor said she couldn't work in her sunny garden anymore.

Poppa gave her pretty cards and sweet letters from all her friends, but Nana didn't feel better.
Poppa read her favorite books, but Nana still didn't feel better.

Poppa made her favorite tea in her prettiest teapot, but that didn't help.

"I don't know what else to do," Poppa said.

I could tell he hurt for Nana. I hurt for Nana, too.

"I think Nana misses her garden," I said to Poppa.
"She misses her flowers.
She misses the butterflies and birds that visit her."

THEN I HAD AN IDEA!

I told Poppa, and he started smiling.
He hugged me hard and said, "Let's do it!"

Dwayne

Do you have a big yard? That's great, but you don't have to have a big yard to be a gardener. Any kind of space will do — a small side yard, petite patio, or tiny terrace will work just fine. Even a sunny window can show off your green thumb when you plan a garden!

• A 2x4 foot space is perfect when your garden is going to grow straight up. That means supporting those trailing vines (such as moonvine, star jasmine, climbing roses, or even veggies and fruits that vine, like some peas, beans, melons, squash and gourds) on a stake so they grow UP, UP and AWAY from the ground.

• Containers — plastic or other material — can be used as your "garden." Be sure to use a soil made especially for potted plants so that it will drain properly and have plenty of nutrition. Choose plants that will be happy with their new home: a plant that likes lots of sun will do best in a sunny spot and a plant that needs plenty of shade will grow best when there is no chance of a sunburn.

Garden Design–
Have a plan!

- What size will your garden be? With a helper, use a tape measure to get the length and width of the space where your garden will be. Multiply those two numbers (the length and the width) together to get the "square footage" to help you decide how much will fit into your garden.

- Draw your new garden on special paper called "graph paper" that has squares on it to make it easier to see where things go.

- What do you want in your night garden? Flowers are nice, but many animals, birds and insects are drawn to plants that also have berries or fruit. Evergreen shrubs make good homes for birds. And animals, birds and insects get thirsty and would love a place to get a drink — like a birdbath or pond.

With shovels and soil and shears,
Poppa and I worked to build Nana's new shadow garden.
We sneaked outside after breakfast every day, moving shrubs and
trimming trees in Nana's old garden. The new plants in our
garden plan needed room to grow.

The new garden needed
special plants – plants that
would sleep while the sun
was high in the sky and
wake up at night.

Alice

"Do you have the seeds?" Poppa asked me.
I patted my back pocket to make sure.

"I'll start digging holes," said Poppa.
"You get the wheelbarrow with our treasures."

I used all of my strength to push that
wheelbarrow – it was so full of plants that
the wheel would barely roll
on the gravel path.

Moon flower seeds

Seeds of knowledge

• Some plants grow well
from seeds, but others do
best if a baby plant is used.

• Plants are made up of many
parts, just like we are. Look
for roots, stems, leaves and
blooms on your plants.

• A seed is a baby plant that
hasn't quite started to grow.
For a seed to start to grow
it needs soil, sun and water.

• If you plant a certain type
of seed, it will grow into
that type of plant. If you
plant a poppy seed, it will
grow into a poppy plant,
not an oak tree!

Romika

Choosing plants for a Shadow Garden...

- choose plants that bloom in the evening, or

- plants that become fragrant at night, or

- plants whose foliage (leaves) and blossoms show up at night, especially in the moonlight. *For example:*

Yuccas

- this plant's foliage shows up at night in the garden

- stiff-leaved, white blooming plant in the agave family

- needs very little water, often grows in desert

- pollinated at night by the yucca moth

- Native Americans and early Americans used yucca leaves for needles, medicine, soap and food

Four-o'clocks

- plant that is named for the time of day its bloom opens

- opening of flower actually triggered by a drop in temperature

- sweet scent released to alert pollinators

- pink, yellow, white or mixed-color blooms; easy to grow from seed.

One plant had sharp leaves.
Poppa told me its name was yucca.

"Let's put the yucca here," I said, pointing at a spot in the open.

I used my hand spade to dig the hole, and Poppa planted it.

ouch, sharp leaves

Yucca Plant

KE-KE

It's HOT out here!

The pink flower we planted
nearby drooped on the ground.

"Look up," said Poppa.
"Feel the sun on your face?
That four-o'clock flower feels it, too.

"Let's finish planting and then water
everything and see what happens."

Poppa dug into the brown dirt,
and I watched the earthworms dance around.

I pulled the hose out and gave the new plants a long drink.

Alejandro

Joseph

dancing earthworms

Poppa climbed high on his ladder. He put little lights in the trees. Then we waited for the sun to go down behind the barn.

Shadows crept out of hiding places all around me.

This night bird is sometimes called a nightjar. Its common name is "Whip-poor-will" because of its call.

• found throughout North and Central America

• sleeps much of the day and comes out at night to eat

• the Hopi tribe of Native Americans' name for this bird means "The Sleeping One"

• lays its eggs in phase with the lunar (moon) cycle, *(see the glossary in the back of this book)*, so that the eggs hatch about 10 days before a full moon comes out.

"Whip-poor-will...whip-poor-will..."

"Whip-poor-will. . .whip-poor-will," something cried over my head.
I grabbed Poppa's hand. "It's too dark," I told him.

"Hold your horses," said my grandfather.
He looked up, cupped his fingers around his mouth and called back.
"It's a bird called a nightjar," said Poppa.

I cupped my fingers around my mouth and cried,
"Whip-poor-will. . .whip-poor-will," just like Poppa.
"Whip-poor-will," the nightjar called back, and the crickets joined in the song.

All of a sudden the
four-o'clock flowers woke up.

Hot pink blooms yawned open.

Moonvines we strung on the garage
wall exploded with blooms like popcorn.
They smelled as good as Nana's
homemade cookies.

A hawk moth zoomed past my head like a helicopter. It flew straight for the yellow evening primroses we planted by the birdbath. The fuzzy moth circled a couple of times, then landed on the petals. A long tongue unrolled and went down into the center of the flower like a straw.

"She's drinking her breakfast," said Poppa.

"How do they find flowers in the dark?" I whispered to Poppa.

"How do you know when Nana's cookies are ready?" he asked.

"Because I can smell," I said.

"They use their antennae instead of a nose to follow the smell," said Poppa.

We watched the big fuzzy moth go to the next bloom.

Allison

Night Insects

Hawk moth
- a large, brownish moth that comes out at night.

- one of the fastest insects, flies over 30 miles-per-hour!

- eats with a "proboscis," an organ on its head that unfurls for sucking the nectar of a flower, much like an elephant's trunk.

Firefly
- beetle that is also called "lightning bug" because of the light shining from its lower abdomen.

- light is actually a chemical reaction that the fireflies use to find one another.

Margaret

Turn that light out, I'm trying to sleep!

I tiptoed toward the barn. In the shadows, I could barely see the little white blooms of the star jasmine by the gate.

The honey whiff I got made me glad I have a nose!

Margaret

Even with the lights on, some parts of our garden stayed dark.
Poppa named these places "listening spots." We dragged the wooden bench
we made last summer into one of those spots and snuggled together on it.
Suddenly something crunched on the gravel path.

Had Nana discovered our secret?

A mother raccoon with her babies slipped by us. She headed toward the old grapevine that hung on Nana's rusty clothesline pole. I knew the vine had juicy grapes. They made my mouth pucker, but Nana made jelly with them that I loved to eat with peanut butter and toast.

"I think they've been here before," whispered Poppa.
We watched mother raccoon plop a grape into her mouth,
then stop to look around.
The babies stood up on their back legs and grabbed
more grapes with their little hands.

They looked so funny in their black fur masks.
Poppa and I laughed. The whole family
waddled away when the mother
made a noise like sandpaper.
"Let's go get Nana," said my grandfather.

Night Animals

Raccoons

- small mammals native to North America, but now found all over the world.
- have their babies in the spring that grow up and are ready to go out on their own in the fall.
- name comes from the Algonquin Indian word ahrah-koon-em, meaning "one who rubs, scrubs and scratches with its hands."

Armadillos

- name is a Spanish word meaning "little armored one." This refers to the hard bony plates that cover the back, head, and legs.
- dig burrows and sleep up to 16 hours per day, looking for food in the early morning and evening: beetles, ants, termites, and other insects.
- have very poor eyesight, but an excellent sense of smell that they use when hunting.

"Nana, we have a surprise for you"

Nana rested in her big bed.
"Nana, we have a surprise for you!" I said.

I held her arm gently and helped her up.
She slid into her soft furry slippers.

"I knew you two were up to something," she said.

Poppa put his big hand under her elbow.

"Where are we going?" asked Nana.

LUIS

"You'll see," said Poppa with a smile.

The screen door squeaked open
to his touch.

Nana looked out and saw her new garden.
Her eyes watered up like mine do when
it's time for me to go home.

She hugged Poppa's neck, winked at me, and slung off her slippers.

Then she tiptoed onto the path, disappearing into her magical new shadow garden.

"Hey, wait for us!" called Poppa.
But Nana didn't even hear him.

She was already gardening in her mind.

More Fun Gardening Facts

Shadow Garden Glossary ~ helpful words to know

Almanac

An annual book that contains information about planting gardens and crops, weather, the phases of the moon and more. One of our country's founders, Benjamin Franklin, printed a famous almanac beginning in 1732.

Anther

The pollen-bearing part of the stamen.

Bats

A nocturnal (active at night) flying mammal with weblike (covered with thin, flexible tissue) wings that extend from their front legs to hind limbs or tail; they navigate using "echolocation," giving out high-pitched sounds and listening to the echoes.

Diurnal

Animals that are active in the day and sleep at night. Many pets (dogs, cats) are nocturnal in the wild but can be trained to become *diurnal* (active during the daytime) like their owners.

Filament

The stalk that supports the anther in a stamen.

Foliage

Plant leaves, especially tree leaves, also considered as a group like a cluster of leaves.

Germinate

To begin to sprout or grow.

Landscape Gardener

A person whose occupation is the decoration of land by planting trees and shrubs and designing gardens.

Moonvine (moonflower)

The Moonvine is in the morning glory family. This vine, native to the tropics, has large white, fragrant blooms and heart-shaped leaves. Soak the hard seeds in water overnight before planting (spring). It is fast-growing (20-30' in a season). Buds open into flowers for only one night, then shrivel and drop the seeds. The juice of moonvine mixed with milky sap ("latex") from trees was used by the Aztecs to make a ball for their famous games.

Nocturnal

Animals that sleep in daylight hours, becoming active during the night, are nocturnal. Most animals who hunt for food at night have specially designed hearing, smell and sight for low light. They usually have dark fur/skin that is not easily seen by enemies. Plants that bloom at night have pollinators that are nocturnal, like the hawk moth.

Owls

Most often nocturnal birds of prey, having hooked and feathered talons, large heads with short hooked beaks, large eyes set forward, and fluffy plumage that allows for almost noiseless flight.

Phases of the Moon

This is the shape of the moon as we see on earth; the shape of the moon does no change at all, but we see it at different angl so it seems to change.

Pollen

The fine powder-like material consisting pollen grains that is produced by the anthe of seed plants.

Soil

A particular kind of earth or ground, like sandy soil. A place or condition favorabl to growth; a breeding ground.

Stamens

The pollen-producing reproductive orgar of a flower, usually consisting of a filamen and an anther.

WEBSITES on Gardening for Kid

- **National Gardening Association**
  www.garden.org
  www.kidsgardening.org

- **Lady Bird Johnson Wildflower Cent**
  www.wildflower.org

- **Junior Master Gardener**
  www.jmgkids.us

- **AgriLife Extension Service – Texas**
  www.texasextension.tamu.edu

- **Native Plant Society of Texas**
  www.npsot.org

Planting by the Light (or dark) of the Moon

Before we had calendars to tell us what time of year it was, the sky was our guide to the seasons.
For hundreds of years, when someone wanted to plant seeds for food, they chose the best time based on
where the moon was in the sky and what it looked like. This is called the PHASE of the moon.
The patterns of the moon's different PHASES are always the same and they run on a CYCLE.
These CYCLES were put into a book in 1639, called an ALMANAC.

We know that the moon is able to cause things on earth to happen, even though it is about 250,000
miles away. (If you could drive around the middle of the earth 10 times, that is about the same distance
the moon and earth are from each other.) Like the earth, the moon has GRAVITY. The moon's strong pull
on the earth – like a magnet – causes the water level on beaches to go up and down, called TIDES.
We also know that when the moon is in a PHASE where we can see the light of the sun reflected off of it,
much like a mirror, it seems that someone has turned on a light for us and we can see further at night
because of the bright light. Some farmers and gardeners believe that those same two powers of the
moon impact their plants: gravity on the water for the plant and the light for making it grow.

So watch the night sky for several clear nights. Do you see all of the moon (a full moon), or none of it
(a new moon)? Is it just a tiny sliver, or a large piece? Then find an almanac at the library and see
what vegetables to plant now and which ones need to wait for a few days.

Where the wild things grow

If possible, select plants that are NATIVE to your area of the world. A "native plant" is one that, according to The Lady Bird
Johnson Wildflower Center, "existed here without human introduction." Native plants are happy with the amount of
water and cold and heat that naturally occurs where they are native. That means that once they are established,
you should not have to give them extra water or protect them from the weather. Native plants are
also less likely to be bothered by bugs or diseases than non-native plants. Besides, the birds and
other wildlife prefer those plants that they recognize and depend upon, ones that have existed
for thousands of years in THEIR backyard.

The Children's Art Project

The process of making a marketable product from a child's simple drawing is a long journey. The journey begins with the art classes where the artwork is created — classes funded by proceeds from the Children's Art Project.

A coordinator and art volunteers teach weekly art classes, which nurture talents and imaginations. The young patients are instructed in a wide variety of art mediums, including watercolor, paint, clay, colored markers and pencils and collage techniques. The time spent creating offers a few moments when a child can focus on something other than the realities of cancer.

All artwork is archived by the Children's Art Project and kept active for many years. Some of the art in this book is new, inspired by educational classroom experiences in the Children's Cancer Hospital. Other art has been previously published before finding a new use in *Our Shadow Garden*. All artwork created by our young patients is saved because we believe that art "waits for the right time."

Pediatric patients in the Children's Cancer Hospital at M. D. Anderson Cancer Center
have many challenges to overcome in addition to fighting their disease.
One of these is to just enjoy being a kid — and that's where
the Children's Art Project steps in.

The Artists of "Our Shadow Garden" Book

 Abdulmajeed
Age 13

 Aida
Age 8

 Aidan
Age 11

 Alejandro
Age 10

 Alexis
Age 9

 Al-Hanoof
Age 15

 Alice
Age 16

 Allison
Age 14

 Amalia
Age 13

 Angelique
Age 12

 Annie
Age 6

 Ashlie
Age 14

 Cesar
Age 8

 Christina
Age 15

 Claudia
Age 9

 Conner
Age 11

 Courtney
Age 15

 Destiney
Age 6

 Dwayne
Age 18

 Elizabeth
Age 13

 Fatemah
Age 11

 Fatima
Age 15

 Greg
Age 14

 Joseph
Age 8

 Jove
Age 14

 Katie
Age 14

 Ke-Ke
Age 12

 Lorenzo
Age 14

 Luis
Age 11

 Margaret
Age 15

 Megan
Age 8

 Melissa
Age 11

 Mercedes
Age 17

 Miguel
Age 8

 Monte
Age 17

 Neil
Age 13

 Nicole
Age 10

 Nik
Age 12

 Ozzie
Age 13

 Rachel
Age 15

 Romika
Age 12

 Sandra
Age 14

 Sayna
Age 15

 Sweety
Age 14

 Terrance
Age 5

 Valesca
Age 6

 Zoe
Age 13

Note: some of the artists listed above have more than one piece of art in this book.

Cherie Foster Colburn is a graduate of Texas Woman's University and is certified by Texas A&M University and the Texas Agricultural Services as a Texas Master Gardener and as a landscape Design Critic by the National Council of State Garden Clubs, Inc. In her landscape design company, Nature's Tapestry, she specializes in low-maintenance design and habitat gardens using native and well-adapted plants. She has worked with schools across Texas designing learning gardens, and teaches landscape design and plant selection for the Texas Agricultural Extension Service and community colleges. She makes television appearances as a native gardening expert and has been published in *Southern Living, Texas Gardener,* and *Houston House and Home magazines,* among others. In addition, Cherie sings alto in a gospel trio, speaks to gardening and spiritual groups, volunteers to create Schoolyard Habitats, develops curriculum, and spends as much time as possible with her plants and critters in The Woodlands, Texas. She and her husband Greg have two daughters, Sarah and Emily.

Our Shadow Garden is the winner of the Southern Writers Literary Award.

For more information about nocturnal creatures and plants or creating your own shadow garden, visit

www.shadowgardenbook.com

M. D. ANDERSON CANCER CENTER
Children's Art Project

The Children's Art Project is a volunteer-driven, non-profit business that funds patient-focused programs at M. D. Anderson Cancer Center. The project focuses on its mission to make life better for children with cancer. This blending of business and emotional elements paints the beautiful picture that is the Children's Art Project. It's a big business … but it comes equipped with a big heart.

www.childrensart.org

bright sky press

2365 Rice Blvd., Suite 202 Houston, Texas 77005
www.brightskypress.com

Proceeds from the sale of this book will fund programs that benefit the educational,
emotional and recreational needs of patients at M. D. Anderson Cancer Center.

10   9   8   7   6   5   4   3   2   1

Library of Congress information on file with publisher.
Printed in the China through Asia Pacific Offset

Requests for permission to reproduce any part of this book should be directed to
The Children's Art Project, P. O. Box 301435, Houston, Texas 77230-1435.
www.mdanderson.org

M. D. ANDERSON CANCER CENTER
Children's Art Project